SMALLER THAN MOST

by Shirley Lincoln Rigby

pictures by Debby L. Carter

Harper & Row, Publishers

For my family

—S.L.R.

Remembering Grammy Belknap

—D.L.C.

Smaller Than Most
Text copyright © 1985 by Shirley Lincoln Rigby
Illustrations copyright © by Debby L. Carter
Printed in the U.S.A. All rights reserved.
Designed by Al Cetta
1 2 3 4 5 6 7 8 9 10
First Edition

Library of Congress Cataloging in Publication Data
Rigby, Shirley Lincoln.
    Smaller than most.

    Contents: Tummy bumps — Grampa helps out —
Smaller than most.
    1. Children's stories, American.   [1. Babies—Fiction.
2. Brothers and sisters—Fiction.   3. Size—Fiction.
4. Pandas—Fiction]   I. Carter, Debby L., ill.   II. Title.
PZ7.R4418Sm 1985   [E]   85-42636
ISBN 0-06-025027-5
ISBN 0-06-025028-3 (lib. bdg.)

 # Contents

Tummy
Bumps

Won-Ton tried to sit
on his mother's lap.
"Your lap is getting smaller
and your tummy is getting bigger,"
Won-Ton said.
Mother hugged Won-Ton.
"I will tell you a story
about my tummy," she said.

4

"Once upon a time
in a forest of bamboo trees,
there lived a mother and a daddy panda
and a little panda.
Mother and Daddy loved their
little panda very much.
But they thought he might be getting lonely.
They thought he might want
another panda to play with."

"Stop, stop," cried Won-Ton.
"I can't listen
to your story anymore."

"Why not?" asked Mother.
"Because your tummy
just bumped me," said Won-Ton.
"That is part of the story,"
said Mother.

"Then keep going," said Won-Ton.
"And maybe the bumps
will go away."
"I don't think so," said Mother.
"Because the bumps
are part of the surprise."
"What surprise?" asked Won-Ton.
"The one in my tummy,"
said Mother.

"There is something inside
your tummy besides you?"
asked Won-Ton.
"Yes," said Mother.
"Someone special.
Someone to love you
and live here with you."
"In my bed?" asked Won-Ton.
"No, not in your bed,"
she said.

"Is it a new panda?"
asked Won-Ton.
"Yes, it is a new panda.
It is a new brother or sister.
And the bumps came from your
brother or sister saying hello,"
said Mother.

"Maybe I can hug your tummy
and say hello back,"
said Won-Ton.
"You can hug my tummy,
but not too hard," Mother said.

9

Won-Ton put his arms
around Mother's tummy
as far as they would go.
"That's just the right hug,"
said Mother.
"Now the new panda
will know you love him."

Grampa
Helps Out

"Grampa is coming today
to take care of you," said Mother.
"Where are you going?" Won-Ton asked.
"I'm going to the hospital," she said.
"I'm going to have the baby."

11

"But Grampa doesn't know anything
about our house," Won-Ton said.
"Then you must help him,"
said Mother.
Just then the doorbell rang.
In walked Grampa.
He brought in three bags.
He hugged everyone.

He whispered in Won-Ton's ear,
"I have some secrets here."
Mother kissed Won-Ton good-bye.
"Take care of Grampa," she said.
Won-Ton waved good-bye.

"Now can I see your secrets?"
he asked Grampa.
Grampa opened all his bags.
There were sticks of wood,
piles of nails, sandpaper, and a saw.
"What are you making?" asked Won-Ton.
"A crib for your baby," said Grampa.
"Can I help? Can I?" asked Won-Ton.
"Of course," said Grampa.
"First find me a hammer and a ruler."
Won-Ton found a hammer and a ruler.
"Now get me a pencil."
Won-Ton ran and got a pencil.
He helped Grampa plan
how the crib would look.
He helped Grampa
measure and hammer.

14

Soon it was time for dinner.
"Find me a big pot," said Grampa.
"I'm making a stew
for the two of us."
Won-Ton found a pot
and carrots, potatoes,
onions, and peppers for the stew.
After eating, Won-Ton said,

"I hear a car. It's Father,
and he'll find the crib.
It won't be a surprise anymore."

16

"Where can we hide it?" Grampa asked.
"In the closet," said Won-Ton.
Grampa grabbed the tools.
Won-Ton grabbed the wood.
They ran upstairs and hid it all in
Won-Ton's closet.

Father came in.
"Mother misses you," he said.
"I miss her too," said Won-Ton.
"When can I see the baby?"
"You can see your *sister* soon," said Father,
kissing him good night.

In the morning when Father left,
Grampa got out the tools.
Won-Ton got out the wood.
After Grampa sawed, Won-Ton sanded.
After Grampa glued, Won-Ton painted.
Before dinner, Grampa hid the crib
in Won-Ton's closet.
When Father came home, he said,
"Mother and the baby come home tomorrow
"Good," said Won-Ton.

In the morning when Father left,
Grampa got out the crib.
He banged in one last nail
to hold a nameplate.
"Ouch," he cried. "I hit my hand!"

Won-Ton ran to the bathroom.
He got a towel and lots of bandages
and ran back to Grampa.
"I'll fix it," said Won-Ton,
wrapping Grampa's fingers in the towel.
"Look, Grampa, no more blood."
"What a good Won-Ton," Grampa said.

19

Just then Mother and Father came in.
Father carried a bundle.
"What happened?" asked Mother.
"Won-Ton took care of me,"
said Grampa.

"So I see," said Mother.
Won-Ton ran to Father.
"Let me see, let me see," he said.
"Sit down," said Father,
"so you can hold your baby sister."

Won-Ton sat down and held his sister.

"What's her name?" he asked.

"Her name is Su-Lin," said Mother.

"Su-Lin," Won-Ton said.

"Grampa and I made you a crib."

Grampa moved the crib closer.

"It's a beautiful crib," Father said.

"It's just right for Su-Lin," said Mother.

"Won-Ton helped a lot," said Grampa.

"So I see," said Mother.

Won-Ton looked at Su-Lin.

"She looks like me when I was little,"
he said.

Grampa peeked at Su-Lin.

"Almost, Won-Ton, almost," said Grampa.

Smaller
Than Most

"Won-Ton, will you watch Su-Lin
while I weed the garden?" asked Mother.
"All right," said Won-Ton.
"Good," said Mother.
"Stay in the kitchen,
and call me if you need me."
"I will," said Won-Ton.
Mother went outside.

"What do you want to do?"
he asked Su-Lin.
"Pot, pot," said Su-Lin,
pointing to the cupboard.
"You want to play pots?" asked Won-Ton.
"Ya, ya," said Su-Lin.

Won-Ton got out two pots and two spoons.
Su-Lin grabbed a spoon
and started to bang on the pot.
"We are making music," said Won-Ton,
banging on the other pot.
"Ya, ya," said Su-Lin.
Suddenly Su-Lin stopped banging.

"Lolli, lolli," she cried,
pointing to the jar of lollipops.
"You want a lollipop?" asked Won-Ton.
"Me, me," said Su-Lin,
crawling to the cupboard.
"I can't reach them," said Won-Ton.
"I'm too small."
"Lolli, lolli," said Su-Lin, starting to cry.

"Stop crying, Su-Lin," he said,
sitting down next to her.
"Lolli, lolli," she said,
pointing to them again.

"All right," said Won-Ton.
"I'll try to get you one."
Won-Ton got a small stool.
He pushed it over to the cupboard.
He got up on his tiptoes and
got a lollipop for Su-Lin.
He got down and gave it to her.
He shoved the stool back.

Just then Mother came in.

"See, see," said Su-Lin,

holding up her lollipop.

"How did she get that?" asked Mother.

"I got it so she would stop crying,"

said Won-Ton.

"Oh," said Mother,

putting Su-Lin in her playpen.

28

Then Mother looked at Won-Ton.
Tears were falling down his face.
"Why am I so small?" asked Won-Ton.
"I'm smaller than most of my friends,
even Chang, and he got a lollipop
for Su-Lin the other day."
"You got her one too," said Mother.
"Yes," said Won-Ton.
"But I needed a stool."

"Show me," said Mother.
Won-Ton shoved the stool
over to the cupboard.
He climbed up on the stool.
"I can reach the lollipops now."
"Get two of them," said Mother.
"One for you and one for me."
Won-Ton took out two lollipops.
He got down and put the stool back.
"Sit here with me," she said,
"while Su-Lin is quiet,
and I'll tell you a secret."
"What's the secret?" asked Won-Ton.
"When I was little like you," she said,
"I was smaller than most of my friends too."
"You were?" asked Won-Ton.
"What did you do?"
"I cried sometimes," said Mother.
"But one day your grandmother
said something that made me feel better."

"What did Grandmother say?" he asked.
"She said never forget that the best
things come in small packages."
Won-Ton laughed.
"I'm glad Grandmother told you that,"
he said.
"So am I," said Mother,
licking her lollipop.